PUFFIN BOOKS

Ambrose
Follows His Nose

Some other books by Dick King-Smith

Contents

PUFFIN BOOKS

UK | USA | Canada | Ireland | Australia
India | New Zealand | South Africa

Puffin Books is part of the Penguin Random House group of companies
whose addresses can be found at global.penguinrandomhouse.com.

www.penguin.co.uk
www.puffin.co.uk
www.ladybird.co.uk

First published 2022

001

Written by Dick King-Smith and Josie Rogers
Text copyright © Fox Busters Ltd and Josie Rogers, 2022
Illustrations copyright © Stephanie Laberis, 2022

The moral right of the authors and illustrator has been asserted

Set in 17/22.25pt Perpetua Std
Typeset by Jouve (UK), Milton Keynes
Printed and bound in Great Britain by Clays Ltd, Elcograf S.p.A.

The authorized representative in the EEA is Penguin Random House Ireland,
Morrison Chambers, 32 Nassau Street, Dublin D02 YH68

A CIP catalogue record for this book is available from the British Library

ISBN: 978–0–241–48840–9

All correspondence to:
Puffin Books
Penguin Random House Children's
One Embassy Gardens, 8 Viaduct Gardens, London SW11 7BW

Dick
King-Smith
& Josie Rogers

Ambrose
Follows His Nose

Illustrated by Stephanie Laberis

PUFFIN

1
A Funny Smell

'That's a funny smell, Mum,' said Ambrose, flaring his nostrils.

His mother raised her head and sniffed the air. 'I can't smell anything funny,' she said.

She turned to the rest of her litter. 'Can you smell anything funny?' she asked.

Ambrose's three siblings raised their heads and sniffed.

'No, Mum,' they said.

Ambrose's mother hopped forward to the wire front of her hutch. 'Roland!' she shouted.

On the opposite side of the shed was another hutch belonging to Ambrose's father, a large white rabbit with red eyes and very long floppy ears that lay upon the floor at right angles to his head. Roland was rather elderly, having come to fatherhood late in life. He was also rather hard of hearing (he blamed this on the shape of his ears), which meant that his family often had to shout at him.

Privately his wife – a pretty little prick-eared rabbit with a soft blue coat, whose name was Woodsmoke – was of the opinion that her husband heard what he wanted to hear and paid no attention to what he didn't.

At this moment he obviously didn't want to hear, as he continued to chew a large carrot without any attempt to answer.

Once again his wife shouted his name, even more loudly, and this time Roland looked up, dropped his carrot, came to the front of his hutch and, with a jerk of his neck, threw one of his long lop ears back over his shoulder and turned his head a little sideways.

'Did you speak, my dear?' he said in his deep voice.

Woodsmoke sighed. She had seen this performance of her husband's so many times; it was a pantomime designed to present to the speaker his 'good' ear. But sometimes it was the left one, sometimes the right.

'Can you smell anything?' she asked.

'Yes, my sweet,' said Roland. 'Carrot. Hay. And, of course, rabbit.'

'No, no. A *funny* smell. Ambrose says he can smell a funny smell.'

'Funny?' said Roland. He stared with his red eyes at the four young rabbits in the opposite hutch.

The first and by far the smallest of the litter was Roly, a little lilac-coated runt named after her father. The second, April, was white with prick ears and bore, in Roland's opinion, a great resemblance to Woodsmoke. The third, Archibald, was plump and grey-blue with lop ears. The fourth was white with grey-blue patches, and had one ear that stuck up and one that flopped down. This was Ambrose.

'When you say "funny", Ambrose, lad,' said Roland, 'do you intend to convey that this

aroma of which you are aware is an amusing
one, calculated to send us all into fits of
laughter? Or do you mean that it is
uncommon, unusual, out of the ordinary,
peculiar?'

'Peculiar, Dad. You see, it's not just one
smell that I can smell; it's a mixture of
several.'

'Such as?'

'Well, there's cat.'

'Nothing odd in that,' said Roland. 'That's the Human – he always reeks of it.'

The rabbits' owner, whose name was Jim Johnson, kept several cats in his cottage. The cats would often snooze on Jim's bed and as a result their smell clung to him, which, though he did not know it, was most offensive to his rabbits.

'Yes, I know that,' said Ambrose, 'but it's stronger than usual. And I think there's another human with him, one that smells of something quite different.'

'Like what?' asked April.

'I can't smell anything,' said Archie through a mouthful of carrot.

'Peppermint,' Ambrose replied thoughtfully. 'And I can smell onions. And bread. And some sort of flower — daisies, I think.'

'Ambrose has a very sensitive nose,' said Woodsmoke with a touch of pride.

'I should think he must have a nose like a bloodhound,' Roland said with a snort.

'What's a bloodhound, Dad?' April asked.

'A hound, my dear, is a dog, and a bloodhound is a breed of dog with an incredibly sensitive nose. If it gets a whiff of something niffy, it can track it for miles and miles.'

'Dad,' said Archie, 'what's "niffy"?'

'Means smelly, dear boy. Pungent. Stinky. Malodorous. Anyway, Ambrose, you must try not to tell fibs. How could any rabbit possibly detect such a mixture of unrelated aromas as onions and bread and cat and peppermint and daisies all at the same time?'

At that moment footsteps were heard outside the garden shed. The door opened and in came the rabbits' owner. In one hand he carried a trug filled with onions and in the other a hunk of stale bread for his pets. Behind him came a small girl. She was holding a kitten and sucking a Polo mint. On her head was a garland made from a daisy chain.

Woodsmoke looked fondly at Ambrose, and bent her head to his upright ear. 'A nose like a bloodhound,' she whispered.

2
Rabbits Just Aren't That Clever

The man set down the trug of onions and opened Woodsmoke's hutch.

'Look here, Biddy,' he said to the girl, 'Woodsmoke's had four new kits!'

Jim Johnson lived alone except for a large number of pet animals. Around his cottage, and sometimes in it, were cats and goats and hens and Muscovy ducks, and there was an aviary full of singing birds, and a very, very old donkey in the orchard.

Biddy was Jim's niece, who had come to stay with him for part of the school holidays. Her visits to the cottage tended to involve a lot of card games, crossword puzzles and bike rides, plus a great deal of puddings. This was no great hardship for Jim. In truth, he and Biddy were mostly interested in the same sort of activities.

Biddy was almost as mad about animals as her uncle. The difference was that he had lots and she had none. Her parents said she was too young to have any pets of her own.

She sighed, peering into the hutch. 'Oh! Uncle Jim, aren't they lovely!'

Since Woodsmoke had produced her first litter a few years before, Biddy had grown very fond of rabbits. When she was younger, and much to Jim's amusement, she had given the shed in which the hutches were kept the rather grand name of Rabbit Hall. After all, Biddy had said, if the birds' house was called an aviary, why shouldn't the rabbits' house have a special name? He couldn't fault her reasoning, and so the name had stuck.

Jim bent forward to give the current inhabitants of Rabbit Hall some stale bread, and the doe and the four young ones recoiled, wrinkling their noses in distaste. Woodsmoke gave a pointed little cough.

'They don't like the smell of that kitten,' said Jim. 'Give it here, love. I'll put it back with the cat. Just watch a minute and see that little lilac runt doesn't roll out of the hutch.'

Biddy stared intently at the litter of young rabbits. *If only Mum and Dad would let me have one of them for my own. Perhaps they will,* she thought, *now that I'm older*, and so thrilled was she at the idea that in her excitement she crunched the mint she had been sucking into little bits.

'If,' she said when her uncle returned, '*if* Mum and Dad would let me, d'you think I could take one of Woodsmoke's babies home, Uncle Jim?'

'Course you could. Which one d'you fancy?'

'That one,' said Biddy, pointing. 'The white and grey one with one ear up and one ear down.'

'Ah,' said Jim. 'Now that's the one I like.'

Biddy's face fell. 'You'll be keeping him then?' she said.

'No, no, I shan't keep any of the youngsters. Only Woodsmoke and old Roland. No, I meant that's the one that

caught my eye. Little buck, he is. I call him Ambrose.'

'Can I hold him, Uncle Jim?'

'Course you can.'

Biddy took Ambrose out of the hutch and cradled him in her arms. On her face was a look of pure delight. On Ambrose's face was a look of pure disgust at the strong smell of cat that still lingered.

Roly, peeking out from beneath a flurry of straw, saw her brother's expression and giggled to herself.

'Look how he's twitching his nose!' Biddy said.

'Yes, rabbits do that,' Jim said. 'They wink open their nostrils to test the air for scent.'

'I know, but Ambrose's nose is much twitchier than any of the others'!' said Biddy.

Jim laughed. 'Perhaps he's got a 'specially good one,' he said. 'Perhaps he's going to be the world's first tracker rabbit, and you can train him to go on a collar and lead and follow trails.'

Biddy's eyes were like saucers with excitement. 'Could I?' she said. 'Could I really?'

'No, love, I'm only joking. A rabbit couldn't do that,' said Jim. He opened the door of the other hutch. 'Look at old Roland here for instance.'

He fondled the big white rabbit's long ears with one hand, and with the other he broke off some of the remaining bread and placed it in the hutch behind Roland's back. Roland's nose twitched madly and he peered wildly about for the food that he could smell but not see. At last he found it and began to eat.

'I'm ever so fond of the old chap, but rabbits just aren't that clever. Not compared to dogs, or pigs, or humans.'

'But, Uncle Jim . . .' said Biddy.

'Yes?'

'Perhaps Ambrose is cleverer than Roland. Please can we try?'

Jim knew that his niece was not likely to give up on an idea once she had her heart set on it.

'All right, love,' said Jim kindly. 'We'll try, just to please you.'

Biddy beamed. She knew that her uncle was not likely to refuse her unless he really had to. Jim Johnson was a creature of habit by nature, but he did like to indulge his only niece.

'OK. You turn your back so's Ambrose can't see what I'm doing,' said Jim, 'and I'll hide this bit of bread somewhere down the other end of Rabbit Hall.'

In half a minute Jim called 'Ready!' and Biddy turned round and put Ambrose down.

The little rabbit put his nose to the ground and without any hesitation lolloped across the floor of the shed to the far end. For a moment he cast about among the clutter of spades and forks and seed boxes and watering cans, velvety nose wiggling, nostrils winking. Then he hopped straight to a big flower pot lying on its side in which Jim had hidden the bread and began to nibble at the food.

'That was amazing!' cried Biddy. 'Wasn't it, Uncle Jim?'

Jim smiled. 'It certainly was, love.'

Biddy regarded her uncle shrewdly. 'You think I'm being silly and it was just a fluke. Well, I don't think it was,' she said solemnly. 'I think Ambrose really is a tracker rabbit. I bet I can train him to track all sorts of things when I take him home.'

'*If* you take him home,' he said, laughing. 'First you've got to ask your mum and dad.'

Biddy sighed. 'Yeah. Dad can't *stand* animals. He's not like you, Uncle Jim.'

'He's not, no.'

'Funny to think you started out like them,' Biddy said, gesturing towards the three young kits in the hutch.

'How d'you mean?' Jim asked. 'Little and hairy?'

'You're still little and hairy,' Biddy replied, nodding at the long ponytail that hung down Jim's back, and which, much to Biddy's delight, he let her plait from time to time.

'Cheeky! But true, I suppose,' Jim said, laughing again. He ruffled Biddy's own mop of tangled hair.

'It's OK, we're all little and hairy round here,' said Biddy, smiling down at the fluffy creature that sat contentedly at her feet, his nostrils still twitching. 'Aren't we, Ambrose?'

3
Roland Rabbits On

When Ambrose had finished his bread, Biddy picked him up and, after a great deal of kissing and cuddling, put him back with his mother and his siblings.

A warning thump from Woodsmoke alerted Biddy to the fact that Roly had almost slipped out of the open hutch door.

'Need to watch this one – always making a break for it, she is. Wouldn't last long out of the hutch with all the foxes 'round here,' Jim said, as Biddy scooped Roly up and deposited her firmly at the back of the hutch.

Once the humans' footsteps had died away, Woodsmoke hissed, 'Roly! You *mustn't* do that again! You wouldn't last long out of the hutch with all the foxes around here, you know.'

Roly scowled. She thought a brush with a fox would be better than being stuck in the hutch day in and day out, but she knew better than to say this to her mother.

'Mum,' April interrupted, 'who was that little human with the Human?'

To Roland and Woodsmoke, of course, Biddy was no stranger. They had seen her before on previous visits. But she was an object of much interest to the young rabbits.

'That,' Roland boomed, 'was the Child. Just as we call a young rabbit a "kitten", so a small human is called a "child".'

Woodsmoke smiled inwardly. *He hears quick enough when he wants to*, she thought to herself.

'This one is a doe child,' continued Roland, 'like our April and little Roly.'

'She took a shine to you, dear,' Woodsmoke said, smiling at Ambrose.

'She seemed very nice,' Ambrose replied.

'She didn't *smell* very nice,' April added.

'Brought plenty of bread, though,' said Archibald as he chomped on a crust.

'Perfectly agreeable, the pair of them,' Roland said. 'The Human does a splendid job of tending to our needs. Why, since I've lived here he's always fed us well, cleaned our houses thoroughly and shown proper respect in terms of grooming and general admiration. I am quite fond of the old fellow, but it's just as well that the work required of him is simple – humans just aren't that clever, you see. Not compared to rabbits.'

'I can't understand what they say,' said Ambrose.

'No kidding,' April said sarcastically, and she let out a stream of odd lilting noises in imitation of human speech, which sent Roly and Archibald into fits of giggles.

'But, of course, dear boy,' said Roland, 'the language of humans is fascinating, but utterly nonsensical. Though the Human *does* say one's name with a proper degree of respect, and that is something one can understand.'

'He mostly keeps himself to himself,' began Woodsmoke, 'but get two or three of them together . . .'

'And they jabber away,' continued her husband, 'nineteen to the dozen. Very odd. It seems humans are lower than us rabbits on the scale of development. Take the matter of perambulation, for example.'

'Perambulation?' said Ambrose.

Behind him, Roly rolled her eyes. She could tell Roland was about to give one of his lectures.

'Yes, perambulation, lad, listen up!
Transporting oneself. Has it ever struck
you just how strangely humans move
around?'

'You mean walking on their hind legs?'
asked Ambrose.

'Precisely. They've never learnt to walk on
all fours!'

'Also,' April said, 'have you ever noticed
that funny fur the Human has?'

'Yes!' Roland
exclaimed. 'You're
quite right. Smooth
as a salmon on top,
with that curious
fluff dangling down
his neck. Like a
horse's tail! Very
primitive creatures,

humans. Small wonder that they try to comfort one another with all those noises.'

'Perhaps they like the sound of their own voices,' said Woodsmoke quietly, and Roly chuckled.

'What's that?' said Roland, flinging back an ear and inclining his head. 'Did you have a pearl of wisdom to add to the conversation, my dearest?'

'I said "I hear the sound of their voices",' replied Woodsmoke sweetly, and the door of Rabbit Hall opened.

'It's not fair, Uncle Jim,' Biddy said dolefully.

She opened Woodsmoke's hutch and took out Ambrose.

She had telephoned her parents to ask if she could take him home when they came

to collect her. The answer had been a
straight 'no'.

'You know I'd look after him properly,
Uncle Jim, and feed him,
and groom him, and clean
him out and everything.'

'I'm sure you would,
love,' said Jim. 'But if your
mum and dad say it's too
much responsibility, well, you'll just have to
be patient and wait till they think you're old
enough.'

'I'll probably be grown up by then,' said
Biddy miserably.

Jim laughed. 'Nonsense!'

In fact, he did not think Biddy's prediction
was nonsense at all. It was true that his
brother Jasper – Biddy's father – had never

liked animals. Jasper was also rather stubborn and was not prone to changing his mind once it was made up. But his niece looked so crestfallen that Jim couldn't bear to crush her hopes any further.

'Perhaps they'll let you next spring, when Woodsmoke has another litter,' he said kindly. 'There's sure to be one among them that will take your fancy.'

'I don't think I could like another rabbit as much as I like Ambrose.'

She held the little rabbit up in front of her face and stared unhappily at him. Ambrose stared back at the Doe Child. The smell of cat was much less strong, he was glad to find, and he was becoming used to peppermint. The Doe Child's eyes looked moist, he noted, and a drop of water came out of one of them and slid down her cheek.

Jim also noticed this. 'Tell you what, love,' he said, 'I'll keep Ambrose here for you. When the other three go to the pet shop, I'll build him his own hutch, and then he'll be here for you, whenever you come to stay.'

'Well –' Biddy rubbed her eyes – 'yes, I suppose that's the next best thing. If I *must* compromise.'

Jim laughed. 'I think so.'

'I'll just have to spend more of my holidays here, so we get enough quality time together.'

'Well, you know I like having you here, love,' Jim said, 'but I think your mum and dad would miss you.'

'Too right!' Biddy said, half joking. 'Just like I'll miss you and Ambrose!'

Despite himself, Ambrose shuddered a little at the sudden blast of peppermint as the Doe Child kissed him on the end of his nose.

'So can I start training him?' she asked.

'Training him?'

'To be a tracker rabbit.'

'Hang on, love, I was only joking about that,' said Jim. And to himself he thought, *There'll be no stopping her now.*

'I know,' said Biddy, her eyes glinting, 'but it'd be fun to try.'

'Well, don't let him loose in the garden. The cats'll have him. You'll have to keep him under control somehow. Tell you what, I've got a little collar and lead somewhere. Let's go and see if I can find it.'

'Can I bring Ambrose?'

'Course you can.'

After the doors of Rabbit Hall had been closed, a babble of talk erupted from the three remaining young rabbits.

'Mum! Mum! Why has Ambrose gone?' April squeaked.

'Why did that Doe Child take him?' Roly demanded with a hint of jealousy.

'Mum,' said Archie, gulping down some hay, 'what's the Doe Child going to do with him?'

'Calm down, all of you,' said Woodsmoke. 'I've never heard such a fuss about nothing. Ambrose is quite old enough to take care of himself, and you are quite old enough not to ask a lot of silly questions.'

To which, she thought, *I do not know the answers.*

Time passed, and Ambrose did not return. Woodsmoke grew just a trifle worried.

'Roland,' she called softly.

There was no answer.

'Roland!' she called loudly.

'No need to shout, beloved,' said Roland. 'Whatever's the matter?'

'It's Ambrose,' said Woodsmoke.

'Who?'

'Ambrose!' shouted Woodsmoke. 'He's not back!'

'No, darling, he's not black,' said Roland. 'As I recall, he's a mixture of white and grey.'

'No, no!' shouted Woodsmoke. 'He's not *returned*!'

'Naturally,' said Roland. 'The Doe Child has taken him away.'

'D'you mean – for good?'

Roland combed his whiskers thoughtfully with one paw. 'Ah!' he said slowly in his most sonorous tones. 'Now that is an interesting use of language. When you ask if Ambrose is gone for good, to whose good are you referring? His own good? The good of the Doe Child? Or indeed – and this is the interpretation that I personally favour – for the good of the rest of us? Which of these alternative meanings –'

He was interrupted at this point by a sharp stamp of Roly's hindfoot, for though she was the smallest of the litter, she had a short temper and a powerful kick.

'Oh, Dad!' she snapped. 'How you do rabbit on!'

4
Biddy Lays a Trail

'I know I put it somewhere,' said Jim, rummaging about in a drawer of the kitchen dresser. 'Ah, here it is! And here's a lead to go with it.'

The little collar he produced was made of leather, with six very small brass studs round it and a very small brass nameplate, which was blank.

'I reckon that'll be just right for him,' said Jim. 'We'd better put his name on it in case he gets lost, shouldn't we?'

'Yes, please,' Biddy said. 'But I shan't ever lose him.'

She put Ambrose down on the kitchen table among the jumble of projects she and Jim had already started: a 500-piece puzzle depicting a very fat sow, a bowl of dough that was proving for the next day's bread, and a sewing machine with a pair of half-sewn dungarees hanging out of it.

'Touch wood,' Jim said, and they each laid a finger on the crowded tabletop.

Carefully, with the sharp point of a skewer, Jim engraved 'AMBROSE' in tiny capital letters on the nameplate.

'There!' said Biddy. 'Your very own collar, Ambrose. What d'you think?' She held it out.

Ambrose sniffed at it. It smelt of mouse. Then to his surprise the Doe Child fitted it round his neck.

His first reaction was to shake his head vigorously, so that his one floppy ear slapped against the tabletop. Then he tried to scratch the collar off with a forepaw and then with a hindfoot, but to no avail.

'It's not too tight, is it, Uncle Jim?' Biddy asked.

'No,' said Jim. 'It's strange to him, that's all. He'll just have to get used to it. He's got no choice. He can't get it off.'

I can't get it off, thought Ambrose. *I've got no choice. I'll just have to get used to it.*

'Mind you,' said Jim, 'he might kick up a fuss when you put the lead on and try to make him follow you.'

But when they went out on to the lawn in front of the cottage and Biddy clipped the lead on to the collar, Ambrose set off immediately on a tour of inspection. There was no question of his following Biddy. She followed him as he lolloped around the garden, his super-sensitive nose telling him about a succession of interesting smells.

Many of these he knew already. Jim grew a great many vegetables and flowers on the land around the cottage, and the fragrance of these often wafted through the window of Rabbit Hall. But there was a host of new smells too that Ambrose followed here and there, towing the Doe Child behind him.

The grass, for example, did not only smell of grass. The lawn was freshly mown and Ambrose's nose reported a lingering scent of petrol fumes and warm oil. Then there was the thin chemical smell of artificial fertilizer, the ancient woody smell of peat around the azaleas and rhododendrons in the shrubbery, and, strongest of all, everywhere was the rich dark brown fruity smell of dung.

Jim fed all his crops, from roses to radishes, with generous helpings from his dungheap, and though the mixture merely smelt like manure to a human nose, it was a simple matter for Ambrose to identify its various components. The cleanings from the rabbit hutches were easy for him, of course, but in addition he distinguished goat pellets and donkey droppings, hen lime and duck muck. Indeed, so sensitive were his powers that, though they were only present in minute quantities, he could even detect the bestowals of budgerigars and the contributions of canaries.

Nothing of this skill was apparent to Jim and Biddy. All they saw was a young rabbit sniffing his way, aimlessly it seemed, around the garden. But plainly this was an enjoyable thing to do, for every now and then the little buck would give a little buck jump.

'What's he doing that for?' asked Biddy.

'He's happy,' said Jim, 'and you're happy watching him, and I'm happy watching you watching him.' He sat down on a garden seat. 'You and your tracker rabbit!'

'He *is* a tracker rabbit,' said Biddy. 'Look at how he found that bread you hid in Rabbit Hall.'

'That was easy,' Jim said. 'He only had to go a couple of metres. A real tracker dog has to be able to follow a long, long trail.'

'How does it know what it's looking for?' asked Biddy, sitting down beside her uncle.

'Well, supposing a dog had to track a person – say you were lost and I was a dog handler with a trained dog – I'd take the dog to the last place you'd been seen, and if I could, I'd show the dog something that belonged to you, something that had the scent of you on it, like a handkerchief, say, or a glove, and I'd let the dog have a good sniff of it, and then off it'd go, following your trail.'

Biddy sat silent for a moment, while Ambrose strained at his lead, anxious to be off in search of new sensations. Then she pulled her hair scrunchie over her wrist and gave it to Jim. 'I'm a lost child,' she said.

'Eh?'

'You hang on to Ambrose,' said Biddy, 'and I'll go off and get lost. Then we'll see if Ambrose can lead you to me.'

'Well, don't go too far, love.'

'I won't,' said Biddy. 'Give me five minutes.'

She handed over Ambrose's lead, and marched off.

Once out of sight round the back of the cottage, Biddy began to lay as difficult a trail as she could devise. *Ambrose will never be able to track me all this way, of course*, she thought. *But just suppose, just* suppose *he did! Wouldn't Uncle Jim be amazed!*

First she walked to the aviary. Then round the duck pond she went (clockwise). Then round the henhouse (anticlockwise). Into the goat shed and out again. Right over the top of the dungheap (she had her wellies on). Then out across the orchard. The ancient donkey was standing, dreaming, under a low crooked apple tree, an easy one to climb. Biddy climbed into it and waited.

Jim looked at his watch. For five minutes he had sat holding Ambrose on his lap, and thinking with fond amusement of his niece and her bizarre notion. In truth, he wasn't wholly surprised that she had come up with the idea of training Ambrose. Whenever Biddy came to stay, Jim's world seemed to open up with strange new possibilities. But really – a tracker rabbit! Pigs might fly.

He stood up, put Ambrose down on the grass and held out Biddy's scrunchie. 'Have a good sniff at this, my boy,' he said.

Ambrose did so.

'Now then,' said Jim, grinning, 'seek! Seek her out, Ambrose!'

Ambrose needed no second invitation. The Human's words meant nothing to him, but after the stench of cat that he had had to endure, the smell of the Doe Child on the scrunchie had come as a blessed relief, and he set off at a steady pace to follow the traces of this scent upon the ground, one ear pricked, one trailing, nose working busily.

Round the back of the cottage he went, pulling Jim behind him, and now Biddy, peering between the leaves, could see exactly where he was going. Which was exactly where she had gone.

First he hopped to the aviary. Then round
the duck pond he went (clockwise). Then
round the henhouse (anticlockwise). Into the
goat shed and out again. Right over the top of
the dungheap (though unfortunately Jim
did not have his wellies on). Then out across
the orchard. Past the dreaming donkey
Ambrose hopped, straight to the foot of the
apple tree.

Here he stopped and, sitting up, began to clean his feet.

Jim scuffed his shoes in the grass. 'There's a mess you've got me in, you silly little chap,' he said. 'And, after all that, you haven't got a clue where she is.' He scratched his head and shouted, 'Biddy! Where are you?'

'Here,' said a voice above his head.

Jim looked up. 'Well, I never!' he said. 'He's found you after all!'

'Yes,' said Biddy, climbing down. 'But what's more, he led you *exactly* the way that I went.'

'Exactly?'

'Yes.'

'Including going right over the dungheap?'

'Sorry, Uncle Jim,' Biddy said sheepishly. 'I was trying to make it as difficult as I could for Ambrose.'

'You certainly did,' said Jim. 'I've never seen anything like it!'

'Ambrose has a very sensitive nose,' she said with a touch of pride.

'Fancy following a trail like that,' said Jim. 'Why, he's a proper little bloodhound!'

'What's that?'

'A breed of dog. One that can track scents for miles and miles. People use them to hunt foxes sometimes, the poor things,' Jim explained.

'How awful!' said Biddy. 'We won't be using you to hunt anything, will we, Ambrose?'

She picked him up, and once again Ambrose found himself staring into the eyes of the Doe Child. There were no drops of water in them this time, he noticed. In fact, they were shining with excitement.

'Uncle Jim says you're a proper little bloodhound,' said Biddy, 'but you can't be that because it's a sort of dog. I'll tell you what you are, Ambrose, shall I? You're not a bloodhound — you're a bloodrabbit!'

5

The Mark of the Bloodrabbit

That evening Ambrose was returned to his family.

'Couldn't he sleep on my bed, Uncle Jim?' Biddy had said.

'No, he could not. Just because he's got a marvellous nose up front, it doesn't mean he's got any control at the back end.'

So that was the end of that – for the time being.

As the Doe Child said her last fond goodnights, the rest of the family stared at Ambrose in shock.

'Just look at Ambrose!' April tittered.

'He's *wearing* something!' Archie chortled, spraying flakes of food about the hutch.

Admittedly it was only a collar. But nevertheless, the sight of a rabbit going about in public wearing anything was – to them – as odd as the sight would be to humans of someone going about in public wearing nothing at all.

Roland guffawed. 'Ambrose, are you wearing a *collar*? What next, I wonder? A shirt perhaps? And then a pair of little pantaloons?'

The kits fell about laughing.

'Oh, calm down, Roland,' Woodsmoke said. 'He could hardly have put it on himself.'

'The Doe Child
fastened it on me,'
Ambrose explained.

'Fascinating!'
Roland said. 'The
Doe Child did it,
you say. Why?'

'I'm not sure,'
said Ambrose. 'She fixed herself to me with a
lead and then she followed me around the
garden. After a bit she got lost. Then the
Human took the lead and followed me, and I
found her, and they both seemed very pleased
with me.'

'Where was she?' Roly asked.

'Up a tree.'

'Up a tree!' Roly whispered. This notion
greatly intrigued her.

'Up a tree!' Roland roared. 'Extraordinary creatures, humans. Needing to be led around their own gardens and then getting lost in them, and up trees at that! How did you find her?'

'I tracked her by scent.'

'I told you Ambrose has a sensitive nose,' said Woodsmoke. 'You scoffed at that, Roland – said he must have a nose like a bloodhound. Well, he must have!'

'Indeed!' said Roland in a jolly voice. 'So you know what he must be, don't you?'

'What must he be, Dad?' Archie asked.

'Ambrose,' said Roland dramatically, 'must . . . be . . . a . . . bloodrabbit!'

The sound of this word, delivered with such apparent solemnity in their father's deep voice, impressed itself strongly upon the young rabbits. As the crown of a king signifies his royalty or the halo of a saint his holiness, so to these rabbits, Ambrose's collar came to be a symbol of an extraordinary personage – a bloodrabbit!

April began to rather fancy a collar of her own. Archie dreamt of the exotic foodstuffs a bloodrabbit would be able to sniff out. And Roly wondered if she, like the bloodrabbit, would be taken to explore beyond the hutch.

Woodsmoke and Roland too marvelled at their son's inexplicable talent. And then came a dazzling ray of light, and after that they never saw Ambrose in quite the same way.

Biddy had got into bed but she was too excited to sleep.

Perhaps he's going to be the world's first tracker rabbit, Uncle Jim had said jokingly about

Ambrose, her Ambrose. But it had turned out to be true!

I must just have a last peep at him, she thought. So she put on her dressing gown, took the torch from her bedside table and crept outside.

The rabbit family was dozing, tired after the day's excitements, and only Ambrose was alerted by the familiar minty smell. Only Ambrose, therefore, was not alarmed when the beam of the torch shone through the window and picked him out, as a spotlight picks out an actor on the stage. But to the others it was an unforgettable and miraculous happening.

One moment the inside of Rabbit Hall was as black as the night without, and then suddenly there came a small perfect circle of brilliant radiance that for perhaps ten seconds

fell full upon Ambrose's motionless figure.
The brass studs on that collar twinkled like
six golden stars.

How wondrous, they thought, how *magical* to
have Ambrose the bloodrabbit in their midst!

6
Ambrose in the Aviary

Next morning, Jim was up early as always to feed his animals. Archie had polished off a large carrot in record time by the time Biddy appeared.

She had enjoyed a deep sleep filled with ambrosial dreams, and had woken feeling very happy. Little did she know what the day was to bring.

With the help of her long-suffering uncle she spent much of the morning training her tracker rabbit. Jim's job was to lay the trail. Ambrose would be given a good long sniff at an object – a pencil, for example – and then Jim would disappear, dragging it along the ground behind him on the end of a length of string. After many twists and turns and criss-crossings he would eventually abandon it in some distant part of the garden or the orchard or among the buildings.

A number of different things were used, some comparatively strong-smelling, like an orange peel or a square of beeswax wrap, and some that smelt to a human nose of nothing at all – Jim's pocketknife, a button, the back-door key.

Each time, Ambrose led Biddy unerringly through every twist and turn and criss-crossing to the end of the trail, and they marvelled at his skill. It did not occur to them that, though he could and did distinguish each individual scent and stored them in his smell-memory, in fact, all he had to do every time was to follow the trail of Jim. There was no mistaking the blend of smells that meant Jim: it was a compound of the man himself and of his clothes to which clung a number of sub-smells, of goat and donkey and various birds, of lavender soap and mint tea, but the principal item was, of course, the reek of cat.

At lunchtime Biddy said, 'I suppose Ambrose can't join us?'

'You suppose right,' said Jim.

'Then I'd better put him back in his hutch.'

'No need to go all the way down the garden if you don't want to, love,' Jim said.

'Stick him inside the aviary. The birds can't hurt him and he can't hurt the birds. He can have a nice chat with the budgies and the canaries.' He grinned at the absurdity of such a notion.

Jim's aviary was a large wire structure with a wooden roof that was joined to the end of the cottage. It was split down the middle by a wire partition. Each side had a shelter with a flight attached: one for the canaries, one for the budgerigars.

'Shan't be long,' she said to Ambrose. 'Be polite to the birds now – you're their guest, remember.' She grinned at the silliness of such an idea.

Jim's canaries, which were of the Yorkshire variety, were at first a little wary of Ambrose. All singing ceased, and the birds peered suspiciously down from their perches at this strange animal.

'Never seen owt like that afore,' said one bird to a second. 'What dost reckon 'tis?'

'Summat strange,' replied the second. Then to Ambrose he said, 'Ey up, lad.'

'Hello there!' Ambrose called from the floor of the flight.

'Buncha drongos, you Pommies! Aintcha niver seen a rebbut before?' said a harsh voice from next door.

The Yorkshire canaries turned their heads to see a green budgerigar hanging on the dividing wire, peering at Ambrose.

'Look, see here, boys!' it shouted. 'Something to remind you of Straya! A dinkum little rebbut with one cronk ear.' And the rest of the budgerigars came flying to see and all began to gabble at once in their noisy way.

'Dost 'ave them in Australia then?' asked the first canary.

'Do we hev rebbuts?' said the green budgerigar. 'We sure do, mite! Heaps of rebbuts, and jumbucks.'

'Excuse me, but what's a jumbuck?' Ambrose said.

'A jumbuck's a sheep, mite,' said the budgerigar. 'What's yer nime anywoy?'

'It's Ambrose.'

'Good onya, Embrose the rebbut! Whatcha doing in the iviary, mite?'

'I don't know,' Ambrose said. 'But I do know I'm hungry. Is there anything to eat?'

'Nobbut birdseed,' said the first canary, 'but tha's welcome to 'elp thaself.'

'I'm afraid I can't eat that,' said Ambrose. 'I only eat things like dandelions and carrots and hay.'

'Strewth, Embrose, you're outta luck thin!' squawked the green budgerigar.

With that he and his fellows flew away, shrieking a shrill chorus of 'Dendelions and cerruts and hie!'

Ambrose looked worried.

'Take no notice of t'owd boodgie,' said the first Yorkshire canary. 'I'd have thowt yon lass would coom and get thee afore long, lad.' No sooner were these words of comfort out of his beak than Ambrose saw Biddy coming. He felt much calmer at the mere sight of her. Little did he know what the afternoon was to bring.

7
Rabbits Go Down Holes

Unbeknownst to Ambrose in the aviary, Roly was just over the hedge in the orchard.

That morning she had at last managed to escape Rabbit Hall.

'Your turn for breakfast now, old boy,' Jim had said to Roland, looking over his shoulder as he closed the door of Woodsmoke's hutch. Had his head not been turned at that exact moment, he would have seen Roly slip

through the gap and plop on to the straw
below.

By a stroke of luck Woodsmoke had not
seen Roly sneak out either. She had been
distracted by the impressive sight of Archie
demolishing a carrot almost as big as he was
and, in the excitement of breakfast and the
Doe Child calling once more for Ambrose,
she had not noticed the absence of her

smallest and most determined kit for quite some time.

'Roland!' she had eventually hissed. After a moment, he tossed his left ear behind him to indicate he was listening. 'Roland, she's done it! She's got out! I *told* her not to; I *told* her there were foxes!'

'Calm yourself, precious one! Who, pray, has got out of where?'

'Roly, of course! She's not in the hutch – I've checked everywhere!' Woodsmoke wailed. 'Oh, Roland, whatever shall we do?'

Roland peered across at his wife's worried face, and the smaller but equally worried face of April beside her. Archie did not look worried at all – in fact, his eyes were closed in what appeared to be a carrot-induced stupor.

'Well, I'm afraid there isn't an awful lot we *can* do, except wait and hope that she is returned to us.' He saw panic flash across the faces of his wife and daughter, and added kindly, 'But perhaps we can try to enlist the help of the Humans in the meantime.'

And so that is what they did.

Now happily nibbling on a fresh dandelion leaf, Roly could not hear the cacophony of thumps coming from Rabbit Hall. The great outdoors, beyond the hutch that was all she had ever known, was more wonderful than even she had imagined. The sights! The sounds! And, though she was not in possession of such a sensitive nose as Ambrose, the smells!

First she had snuffled between the shrubs. Then she had hopped, skipped and jumped up the path. She hid behind a rock when she spotted Jim's old ginger cat, and made a dash for the orchard once the coast was clear. She frolicked at the feet of the donkey, and gambolled in the long grass beneath the apple trees.

Free at last! I must be the happiest rabbit there ever was, she thought to herself. So enchanted was she that she didn't even notice the familiar sound of the approaching Doe Child's chitter-chatter.

Then Roly spotted a huge hole in the ground to her left. She bounded closer, noticing a rather strong smell emanating from it. Some instinct deep within Roly, inherited from her wild ancestors, told her that rabbits go down holes. And so that is what she did.

*

Biddy carried Ambrose into the orchard. She put him down on the grass, holding on to his collar, and was just about to clip on the lead when it struck her that it would be a treat for him to have a little time free. Her uncle believed in 'free-range' animals, by which he meant that his various pets should be allowed to wander as they pleased, as long as they weren't in danger. Biddy was very much in agreement with this philosophy. Indeed, she rather enjoyed being a free-range child when she came to visit.

Don't let him loose in the garden, Uncle Jim had said. *The cats'll have him*. But this wasn't the garden, Biddy reasoned, where Ambrose might escape from her into the shrubbery or under one of the sheds, and there were no cats in sight, nothing at all, in fact, except the old donkey drowsing in a corner. There was just plenty of good grass. *Which is just what a tracker rabbit needs*, she thought. She unclipped Ambrose's lead and he began to graze contentedly. Every now and then he would lollop along a few metres to a fresh patch, while Biddy walked beside him, confident that she could catch him whenever she wanted to, and enjoying him enjoying his freedom.

So they moved across the orchard, pottering happily together in the sunshine. They came upon a patch of daisies and Biddy sat down in the grass with her tracker rabbit by her side. Birds sang, Ambrose nibbled and Biddy daydreamed.

Two scents stood out to Ambrose from the moment they had entered the orchard: one was very strong and, frankly, utterly disgusting. The other was much gentler and reminded him intensely of the hutch that was his home. It was not until a little later, when he saw a flash of lilac fur among the grass that he realized precisely what – or who – it was.

'Roly!' he cried in excitement, bounding towards her.

But she had vanished.

When Biddy opened her eyes, after what felt like a split-second, she saw Ambrose lolloping away. She lunged for him, missed and

scrambled to her feet. 'Ambrose! Come back!'

But he had disappeared down a large hole in the side of the bank.

'Ambrose!' cried Biddy in panic. 'No!' She ran forward and, dropping to her knees, put her head down and peered in.

There was nothing to be seen of him, but there was a strong smell coming from the mouth of the hole, and even Biddy's poor senses told her that it was not the smell of rabbit. It was a rank and most unpleasant smell.

It was the smell of fox.

8

Foxes Are Extremely Fond of Rabbits

Inside the hole, the musky smell was even more pungent. Though Roly's wild ancestors could have told her what it was quick enough, it meant nothing to her. True, she did not care for it – it was not at all nice – but it did not spell danger to her.

As Roly progressed deeper, past several side tunnels, the smell became stronger and she sneezed loudly.

'Bless you!' said a voice behind her.

Roly spun round in surprise. There, silhouetted against the traces of light that filtered down from the world above, was a figure. A huge figure, it seemed to Roly: perhaps ten times her size, reddish in colour, with a long pointed nose and a pair of sharply pricked ears. The stink of it was overpowering.

Roly had a terrible realization. She had never seen one of these animals before, but she had certainly heard a lot about them. She sneezed a second time.

'Bless you!' said the animal again. 'I trust you have not caught cold? It gets draughty down here and there are problems with rising damp. A cold can so easily lead to pneumonia, and it would be a shame to cut short so promising a young life, wouldn't it?'

'I haven't got a cold,' said Roly indignantly. Then she remembered who she was talking to, so through gritted teeth she added, 'I think some dust got up my nose. Thank you for asking.'

'What a nice little rabbit!' said the creature. 'A bit on the small side admittedly, but tender — tender-hearted, that is to say — and polite into the bargain. In fact, you might be the politest, sweetest little rabbit I've ever met. And I've met *a lot* of rabbits in my time.'

Roly tried not to scowl. She did not like to be patronized.

'I'm a fox, you see,' he continued. 'And foxes are *extremely* fond of rabbits.'

'F-fond of them?' Roly replied, trying to stop her voice from quavering.

'To eat,' said the fox.

*

Above ground, Biddy had acted pretty sensibly. Though she could well imagine the danger that Ambrose was in should the occupant of the fox earth be at home, she did not lose her head.

If I was Alice in Wonderland, she thought, *I could go down the hole after Ambrose. But I'm not.*

And if he were trained, like an obedient dog, he'd come out when I call. But he isn't.

So I must get help. But I don't want to run off to fetch Uncle Jim because Ambrose might come back up. So I must shout.

Jim was fertilizing the artichokes in his vegetable patch when he thought he heard a distant cry. It sounded like Biddy's voice, and he hurried into the orchard. He could now see his niece waving her arms, and he could hear what she was yelling.

'Help! Uncle Jim, HELP!'

'What's the matter?' he shouted.

'Ambrose is down a fox hole!'

Jim grabbed his spade and ran.

Underground, Roly had no need of any instincts from wild ancestors to tell her of her peril. At the fox's words she turned and bolted, but almost immediately bumped her nose against a solid wall of earth.

'Dead end,' said the fox.

Thoughts raced through Roly's brain. This was exactly the danger her mother had warned her of. No matter how loud she squealed – which was what her wild ancestors' instincts told her to do – her family would not hear her. All she could do was fight for her life. She set her back against the earth wall.

Suddenly a voice cut through the darkness.

'GET AWAY FROM HER!'

The fox spun round, giving Roly a full view of the owner of the voice.

Ambrose! She had never been happier to see those madly fluttering nostrils and lopsided ears.

'Another one!' chuckled the fox. 'This is turning out to be quite the family affair. Not as polite as your sister, are you? Get away from her, *or what*?'

'Or – or you'll regret it! I'm not an ordinary rabbit, you know!'

'I can see that,' said the fox. 'Your ears don't match, your nose is twitching like you've smelt a ghost, and you're wearing a collar like a dog. What kind of rabbit are you then?'

'I,' said Ambrose, 'am a BLOODRABBIT!' and he gave the fiercest growl he could manage.

Roly held in a giggle. It was not the most intimidating display.

'Are you indeed?' said the fox, sounding, Ambrose thought, rather impressed.

'I'm rather impressed,' said the fox. 'I've no idea what a bloodrabbit is, but I admire your pluck, I must say. Never met one like you

before, or your sister for that matter. In fact,
I think that this is the moment to set your
minds at rest. Relax. Take it easy. Today's your
lucky day.'

Roly, never one to mince her words, cut in.
'Do you mean you're not going to eat us?'

The fox gave a little sigh. 'That's exactly
what I mean,' he said.

'Why not?'

In reply the fox opened his jaws wide.
Apart from the odd broken stump, there
wasn't a tooth in his head. He shook it sadly.
'Old age, young fellows, old age. *Change and
decay in all around I see*, especially in my
gnashers. My bark, I fear, is immeasurably
worse than my bite. A great pity, for the very
sight of you makes the mouth water, but I'm
afraid I just couldn't manage to.'

'Manage to what?' Roly demanded.

'Chew you.'

'Oh,' said Ambrose. 'Oh, good.'

'So, unless bloodrabbits eat foxes –'

'Oh, they don't!' said Ambrose.

'We might as well be friends,' finished the fox. 'What's your name?'

'Ambrose. And this is my sister, Roly.'

'Oh yeah?' The fox smirked. 'What's that short for – Casserole?'

'No! Mum and Dad thought I was a boy, so they called me Roland,' Roly said matter-of-factly. 'But I'm a girl. So now I'm Roly.'

'How fascinating. I don't use my original name either, you know.

My name's Nigel, but for some reason everyone uses my nickname.'

'What's that?' said Roly.

'Niffy,' said the fox. 'I can't think why.'

9

Nice Not Eating You

'It's a nice name,' said Roly, straight-faced.

The fox looked pleased. He grinned at them, flashing his toothless gums.

'D'you really think so?' he said. 'What a decent little rabbit you are, to be sure.'

Outside Biddy was still yelling.

'That kid belong to you?' asked Niffy.

'Yes. She does,' Ambrose said firmly.

'And what d'you suppose is the matter with her?'

'I expect she's lost,' said Ambrose. 'It's funny actually; they seem to get lost all the time. Even on their own property! Then I have to find them.'

'Them? There's more than one?'

'There's a big human as well.'

'How do you find them?'

'By scent,' Roly explained. She felt a sudden rush of pride for her brother. 'He tracks them. He's a good tracker.'

'Oh, now I get it! That's why you call yourself a bloodrabbit.' Niffy shuddered. 'Sooner have you than a bloodhound any day, Ambrose my friend. I've seen enough hounds to last me a lifetime. By the way, has this human got a dog?'

'No.'

'Good. Then there's no great hurry. We can have a nice chat. I never have anyone to have a good natter with nowadays. I'm only sorry I haven't anything in the way of food to offer you. In times past there'd have been sure to be a wing of chicken lying about, or a leg of –' he paused with the word 'rabbit' on the tip of his tongue – 'um, rat.'

'Actually, we don't eat that sort of stuff,' said Roly. 'Only vegetables and, of course, grass.'

'Grass? Yuck!' said Niffy. 'I only eat grass to make myself sick. Meat's the thing. I couldn't do without meat.'

'But, Niffy,' said Ambrose, 'how do you manage without any . . .' He paused, embarrassed.

'Choppers?' asked Niffy.

'Well, yes.'

'Easy,' said Niffy. 'Boring, but easy. I live on a diet of worms.'

'Worms? Yuck!' said Roly.

'Well, I need to have something I can gulp straight down, you see. Beetles are OK and grubs and birds' eggs if I can get 'em, but mainly it's earthworms. Trouble with swallowing them whole is that it takes a bit of time for the digestive juices to kill 'em. They wriggle around a bit in the old tum. Gives me awful wind.'

Before Niffy could go into further details, there was a dull thump overhead, and a few grains of soil fell on them from the roof above.

Jim had wasted no time above ground. He saw the lead dangling from Biddy's hand but made no comment. Instead he dropped to his knees, squinted into the hole to gauge the direction it took, and then climbed on top of the bank. A couple of metres in from the mouth of the fox earth, he drove in his spade and began to dig straight down.

Small though he was, Jim was strong and an experienced digger. His spade was sharp, the ground sandy and softish, and before long he was knee-deep in the oblong hole he was cutting out.

If only a bloodrabbit looked as fearsome as it sounded, he thought grimly, *we might have a chance of getting him back in one piece.*

Underground, Niffy pointed his muzzle towards the ceiling. The thump of the spade sounded close now.

'Time I was off,' he said. 'It's been a pleasure to meet you two but I've no desire to meet your humans. So, if you'll excuse me, I'll slip away now and they need never know I was here.'

Roly wrinkled her nose. *Even humans,* she thought, *couldn't miss this pong,* but all she said was, 'Won't they see you leaving?'

'Back door,' said Niffy. 'Bolthole that comes out in the wood. So long, Roly and Ambrose the bloodrabbit. See you again one day perhaps.'

'I hope so, Niffy,' said Ambrose. 'It's been nice meeting you.'

The fox gave his gummy grin. 'And it's been nice not eating you,' he said, and with a whisk of his brush tail he turned and vanished up a side tunnel.

Ambrose and Roly looked at each other.

'Well, that was fun,' Roly said, grinning.

'Roly,' Ambrose said, shaking his head in disbelief, 'how on earth did you end up here?'

'I've been exploring,' she said shortly and ambled past him, back towards the hole through which they had both entered.

*

A moment later, Jim's spade broke through the roof.

So deep had he now dug that all Biddy could see of him was the top of his bald head each time he threw out a spadeful.

He straightened up, mopping his streaming brow.

'I'm sorry, love,' he called. 'I'm afraid Ambrose has had it. Or, rather, the fox has had *him*.'

Suddenly Biddy felt something soft nuzzling at her ankle.

'You must try to be brave,' Jim said. 'He's in a better place now.'

'I will,' said Biddy. 'He is – and so's his sister!'

10
A Piece of Cake

After a fretful day of waiting, the rest of the family were very glad when Biddy brought both Roly and Ambrose back to the hutch. They claimed to have been together the whole time, which Woodsmoke could not disprove, though she had her suspicions.

Relieved though they were to see the pair, the rabbit family could not ignore the very strong scent that clung to them.

'What's that horrible pong? Have you two been rolling in something?' said April, wrinkling her nose.

Archie reared his head from the food bowl and groaned. 'Bleeeuurgh! That smell's really putting me off my food.'

They, of course, had no experience of foxes, having led a sheltered life. But Roland and Woodsmoke knew. They had lived in Rabbit Hall much longer, and on several nightmarish occasions had smelt that dreadful smell and seen, through the window, a long-nosed figure skulking in the darkness.

As the scent reached him, Roland gave a series of warning thumps with his hind feet. 'Fox!' he growled. 'They stink of fox!'

'We've just met one,' said Roly casually.

Archie and April goggled.

'*Met* a fox!?' Roland bellowed. Then he remembered the miraculous light that had shone in the darkness. He felt once again, and more strongly now, that this strange son of his was not as other rabbits were.

'Met a fox, you say?' he said again, but quietly now.

'Yes,' said Ambrose. 'I – I mean, we – went for a walk with the Child, you see, and there was this hole, and I – I mean, we – went down it, and a fox named Nigel lives there, only everyone calls him Niffy.'

Roland shook his head in bewilderment, and his long ears slapped against the floor of his hutch.

Woodsmoke rounded on them. 'How many times have I told you it's not safe out there?! Foxes *eat* rabbits!'

Archie and April gasped.

'Not this one, Mum,' Roly said calmly.

Ambrose looked round at the faces of his family. On each was a kind of respectful wonder. He opened his mouth to explain that Niffy was toothless and was more keen on a pleasant chat than a rabbit supper, when Roly butted in.

'Because,' she said, 'this fox wouldn't *dare* eat a bloodrabbit!' And she turned to Ambrose and winked.

In the cottage Jim, thirsty after so much digging, was drinking tea, and Biddy, hungry after so much worry, was eating cake.

'I told you, Biddy, didn't I?' said Jim in as severe a voice as he could manage. 'I said right from the start – don't let him loose.'

'I'm sorry, Uncle Jim,' said Biddy in as penitent a voice as she could manage.

'And I'm sorry you had to do all that digging for nothing.'

'Not to worry, love,' said Jim. 'We must be careful with that little lilac one, though. I haven't a clue how she got out.'

'I suppose,' Biddy said, grinning, 'it's not such a bad thing Ambrose was off the lead after all. Else he might not have been able to save his sister, isn't that right, Uncle Jim?'

'I suppose so,' he said, laughing. 'But it would have been a very different story if that old fox had been at home.'

'Perhaps he was,' Biddy said thoughtfully. 'Perhaps he went out of his back door when you started digging.'

'What, you mean the fox and the rabbits had a nice little chat and then the fox said, "So

long, chaps, see you again one day perhaps?"
Pull the other one, love. Foxes, in case you
didn't know, *eat* rabbits.'

'Perhaps,' Biddy said, 'foxes *don't* eat
bloodrabbits.'

Jim smiled. 'You and your Ambrose,' he
said. 'He's just your cup of tea, isn't he?' And
he poured himself another one. 'You're
going to have to say goodbye to him at the
end of the week, though, love. Or rather "*au
revoir*".'

'What's that mean?'

'"Till I see you again." Till next time you
come to stay.'

'I shan't half miss him.'

'I expect he'll miss you too. I'll have to
make sure he doesn't get loose again or he
might set off and track you all the way home.

After all, it's only fifty miles. Easy for a
tracker rabbit, I imagine?'

'A piece of cake!' said Biddy, and she cut
herself another one.

11

One Clever Bunny

Over the next few days Biddy and Jim laid a few more trails for Ambrose, but they were careful not to let him off the lead. Instead of the strict training regime Biddy had originally had in mind, they spent more time playing with all the kits together, and the rest of the week passed with a great deal less peril. In fact, it turned out to be Biddy's best visit yet.

On Tuesday Jim showed Biddy how to milk the goats and make cheese by curdling the milk with lemon juice.

On Wednesday they packed a picnic and went for a long bike ride. Biddy took the binoculars that Jim had given her for her eighth birthday and, to her delight, spotted a buzzard.

On Thursday it rained, so they lit the fire in the cottage and stayed in. Jim helped Biddy finish sewing the dungarees he had started for her – to match his own pair – and they played many games of chess (which Biddy won) and Scrabble (which Jim won).

Before they knew it, it was the end of the week. Biddy slept fitfully that Friday night. Perhaps because she knew she must leave Ambrose soon, her sleep was filled with dreams about him, and one of them turned into a kind of nightmare. In it she opened the door of Rabbit Hall and found only two rabbits – Roland in his hutch and Woodsmoke in hers – and she ran to find her uncle, crying, 'Where's Ambrose?'

'Who's Ambrose?' he said.

'Ambrose! My tracker rabbit! You said you'd keep him for me!'

'Did I say that?' said Uncle Jim in the dream. 'Fancy! I'd quite forgotten. I'm afraid I've sold the lot.'

'That's what you said,' she told him at breakfast time. ' "I'm afraid I've sold the lot." '

Jim grinned. 'Don't you worry, love,' he said. 'Like I said, I'll be taking the other three to the pet shop when you leave, but then I'll build your precious tracker rabbit a nice hutch of his own.'

After breakfast they set about preparing for the arrival of Biddy's parents. The first job was to get the house in order.

Jim's cottage only had one spare room, which was big enough to fit a single bed and not much else, though the walls were covered with various photographs and artworks from Biddy's previous visits. This was where Biddy slept when she came to stay, and both she and Jim privately thought of it as her room.

Biddy's parents would sleep in what was supposed to be the dining room. Like most parts of Jim's home, the dining room was used to house various animals: mice, injured birds, kittens – just not all at once. Jim preferred to entertain guests, when he had them, in the kitchen.

'Now, Biddy,' Jim said from behind a tower of moth-eaten pillows. 'Your dad doesn't like

animals and I can't say as I understand why, but he's my guest so we'd best get this place nice and clean for him.'

'Yes, sir!' Biddy said, standing to attention, broom in hand.

First they moved all traces of animals – bowls and bird feeders, cages and cat beds – from the cottage into Rabbit Hall or the goat shed. Then they scrubbed, swept and dusted, and finally they made up a bed with Jim's best linen and plumped the pillows.

'Good as new!' said Jim, beaming.

The second job was to prepare dinner. Jim, fond of animals as he was, preferred not to eat meat, and neither did Biddy when she came to stay. They raided the vegetable patch and readied a feast: a quiche with leeks and the goat's cheese, new potatoes with mint, roast beetroots of deep magenta and fat broad beans popped straight from their shells.

'Got a challenge for you,' Jim said to Biddy, heaving a vast tub of red berries on to the table, 'like they do on that baking programme you like. See if you can follow this recipe your granny wrote down years ago – it was your dad's favourite pudding when he was your age.'

'Never heard of it,' Biddy said, studying the red-splattered recipe. 'But I'll give it a go!'

Once all the chores were done, they set up the rabbit run on the lawn so that the kits and their mother could potter freely in the grass. Biddy lay next to them, several books spread out on a tartan rug.

'Oh, Ambrose,' she said, idly poking marigolds through the chicken wire. 'If only we could stay like this forever.'

By way of
response Ambrose
lay back with his legs
in the air and closed
his eyes.

'Well, I'm glad
you're taking things in your stride at least.'
Then Biddy sighed, and she tried to put
thoughts of leaving her rabbit out of her
mind.

At three o'clock on the dot, which was
exactly the time at which they said they
would arrive, Biddy's parents pulled into
Jim's driveway.

Usually Biddy would be glad to see them,
but on this occasion their arrival meant only
one thing. She would be going home
tomorrow, and unless some kind of miracle

occurred, she would not be taking Ambrose with her.

Biddy's father Jasper and his brother Jim had the same greeny-brown eyes. Bottom-of-the-duck-pond colour, their mother had called it. They also had the same dimples (left cheek only), the same bushy eyebrows, the same crooked front teeth and the same spray of freckles across the bridge of the nose.

That, however, was where their similarities ended. Jim wore spectacles; Jasper preferred contact lenses. Jasper's hair was cropped all over; Jim grew his long. Jim lived in his scruffy dungarees and knitted jumpers; Jasper always wore a neatly pressed shirt tucked into a pair of neatly pressed trousers. In fact, Biddy had never seen him wear anything else, except at the beach.

Jasper stepped out of the car, followed by his wife.

Biddy's mother, unlike Jasper and Jim, was rather tall, and always wore her long hair bundled atop her head like a prize cabbage. This made her look even taller. She was a cuddly sort of woman, and she immediately pressed her only daughter to her bosom and covered her head in kisses.

'Afternoon, Jim,' said Jasper, extending a hand towards his brother. 'I hope Biddy hasn't been too much trouble.'

'Not at all, Jasper, not at all!' replied Jim, winking at Biddy. 'Just the right amount of trouble, I'd sa–' But he too found himself smothered in an enormous hug, with a kiss planted squarely on the small bald patch on top of his head.

This must be how Biddy makes poor Ambrose feel, he thought.

'Dear Jim!' cried Biddy's mother. 'Thank you ever so much for looking after Biddy. She does love it here, don't you, darling?'

Biddy smiled sweetly and nodded.

'Always a pleasure, Mona,' Jim said, realizing just how much he would miss having Biddy around. He tried to put the thought out of his mind. 'Shall I put the kettle on?'

Once the tea was finished, Biddy's father unpacked the car. Packing and unpacking cars was an activity he took very seriously. Then they all went for a walk through the surrounding fields. Biddy skipped along, telling her mother all about Ambrose and his remarkable powers, while Jasper and Jim strolled behind in companionable silence.

'. . . and he led poor Uncle Jim straight over the dungheap! And he didn't even have his wellies on!' Biddy giggled.

'This Ambrose sounds like one clever bunny,' Mona said cheerfully. *And one you're very attached to*, she thought. She shot her husband a meaningful look.

'A clever bunny. Yes, quite,' he said. *And one Biddy's far too attached to*, he thought.

'The cleverest!' said Biddy. 'When we get back we'll show you just how he does his tracking.'

'He is quite the little tracker rabbit,' Jim added.

At this last word Jasper rolled his eyes. 'I don't know that we'll have time for that, Biddy,' he said. 'You'll need to pack your things this evening before we have supper.'

'After dinner then,' said Biddy.

'We won't want to handle a smelly old rabbit straight after we've eaten, Biddy.'

'He's not old; he's a young buck! And he is smelly, but not in the way that you mean,' Biddy muttered. She could tell from her father's expression that she would do well to leave it at that.

The meal was a great success, and they washed it down with Jim's elderflower champagne (elderflower cordial for Biddy). While Jim was washing up, a chore he rather enjoyed and never had reason to do much of, Biddy unveiled her masterpiece: a huge oozing summer pudding.

'Delicious!' Jasper proclaimed. 'Best I've had in years. You know, Biddy, this was my favourite pudding when I was your age.'

'Funnily enough, Dad, I did know that,' Biddy said, smiling. 'A dicky bird told me.'

After dinner they played cards and Jim insisted on opening the bottle of whisky that Mona had brought him.

Before long, Biddy felt her eyelids drooping and took herself to bed, entirely unaware that she would not be spending much time there on this particular night.

12
A Fox Calls

Late that night, Niffy made his way back to his earth to find it wide open to the moonlit heavens. By the edge of the long hole that Jim had dug, the old fox sat belching gently (for he was very full of earthworms) and thinking about that week's events. He felt rather unhappy.

He was not greatly worried about the ruin of his home. The place was of no use now that those humans, whose smell he found so unpleasant, knew of it. He had other places to sleep, and indeed had spent the last few days laying low in one such hole.

No, what had saddened him, he realized, had been parting from those nice young rabbits. *It's been ages*, he thought, *since I exchanged a single word with a fellow animal, and I did enjoy chatting to the little chaps.*

I could do with a friend, thought Niffy, *I'm old and I'm lonely*, and he pointed his long nose at the stars and gave a string of sharp sad barks.

Usually the sound of the fox's yaps would wake Jim, protective as he was of his beloved ducks and chickens and rabbits. Tonight, though, full of pudding and whisky, he slept like a log.

'That fox'd . . . better stay . . . away . . . our rabbits,' he mumbled. Then he rolled over and fell into an even deeper sleep.

Out in Rabbit Hall the rabbits heard the barking and Roland thumped the floor of the hutch.

'*That's* a bad sign,' April announced matter-of-factly.

'What is it, Dad?' cried Archibald, hiding behind one of his own ears.

'It's probably Ambrose and Roly's foxy friend,' said Roland sourly. 'The one that doesn't eat bloodrabbits. But he'd eat you lot quick enough if he could.'

'No, he wouldn't,' said Roly.

'Roly!' Woodsmoke snapped. 'Don't contradict your father! Just because you got to roam free for a day, doesn't mean you know more about foxes than him.'

'Well said, my dear,' Roland murmured.

'I know more about this one,' Roly muttered.

'Don't worry, everyone,' Ambrose said cheerfully. 'I can smell him from miles off. As a matter of fact I can smell him now! I'll let you know if he gets any closer.'

Ambrose had become accustomed to his family treating him with a certain level of respect but for once none of them looked impressed.

The barking woke Biddy from her slumber. The luminous face of her watch told her it was just after midnight.

That's it then, she thought gloomily. *Today's the day I have to leave Ambrose.* A tear rolled down her cheek and on to the pillow.

She tossed and turned. *I'll never get back to sleep while I feel this miserable*, she thought. She sighed. Then she made up her mind.

Just as she had done a few nights before, she grabbed a torch, crept down the stairs and headed for Rabbit Hall.

Second time round, the rabbit family were less enchanted by the miraculous beam of light and the familiar figure that followed it.

Biddy retrieved Ambrose swiftly and fastened the door. Remembering Jim's warning, she double-checked that Roly had not rolled, or indeed leapt, out of the hutch.

Ambrose, startled at first, was comforted by Biddy's gentle minty scent as she carried him back to her room, tiptoeing all the way.

She was determined to make the most of her last precious hours with her tracker rabbit. First they played a few rounds of Hunt the Polo Mint. Then Biddy lay down while Ambrose ambled here and there, taking in all the new smells.

'Come on, Ambrose,' she said, yawning. 'Hop up here and get comfy.'

This he did, and before long both Biddy and Ambrose were fast asleep.

One might assume, judging by the amount of sleeping they do during the day, that rabbits are nocturnal. In fact, rabbits are what we call crepuscular creatures, which means they are most active around dusk and dawn.

As such, the whole rabbit family had been sleeping soundly when Biddy appeared. They were used to seeing the Humans only during daylight hours and being left well alone the rest of the time.

April yawned. 'Mum, why's the Doe Child taken Ambrose in the middle of the night?'

'I don't know, dear, but I'm sure he'll be fine,' Woodsmoke replied, though she was not.

'Mum,' Roly whispered, sidling up to her mother, 'I could go and look for him –'

Woodsmoke sighed. 'How exactly do you intend to do that, Roly?'

Roly looked rather sheepish. She hopped forward, rooted around in the straw and revealed to her mother a small hole where the chicken wire met the wooden frame of the hutch. A hole certainly too small for a normal-sized rabbit, but just big enough perhaps for a very small rabbit to wriggle through.

Woodsmoke looked furious. 'Roly,' she whispered, 'I don't know how you've done

this, but it's *not* big and it's *not* clever!'
Privately she thought it was actually very
clever indeed, for Roly had made the hole in
a spot the Human was unlikely to notice, far
from both the hutch doors and the feeding
bowls.

'I don't know what good you think *you*
looking for Ambrose will do – he could be
anywhere, and you can't exactly track him
down! Besides, there's a reason we live in a
hutch! It's dangerous out there, Roly; you
have to find your own food and never mind
the *fox* –'

At that moment Archie interrupted them.
'Mum, why's that awful smell back?'

At this Roly gave a start. Archie was right:
the familiar stench of fox, and not just any
fox but a particular flatulent fox, hung in
the air.

'Oh,' Woodsmoke said very quietly. 'Oh dear.'

There came a faint scratching at the door of the shed. For once Woodsmoke did not need to shout at Roland to get his attention.

The scratching got louder. Roly could see her father's large red eyes widen, luminous in the dark.

Roly gave a huge sniff. Satisfied that what or who – she could smell was what – or who – she thought it was, she drew breath, and at the top of her little lungs shouted, 'NIFFY!'

'Roly!' came a muffled voice. The scrabbling stopped. 'That you, old chum?'

Woodsmoke, Roland, April and Archie looked at Roly with horror.

'It's me, Niffy! It's Roly! Niffy, we need help! The Humans have taken Ambrose in

the dead of night and we don't know where
he is!'

'What a cheek! Think they own the place,
that lot. Want me to go and have a look for
him?' Niffy replied through the door.

'Oh, yes please, Niffy!' Roly shouted back.
'We'd be ever so grateful.'

'Anything for the bloodrabbit, eh? I'll be
back before you can say "Jack Robinson".'

They heard the patter of foxy footsteps fade
away and with them, mercifully, the terrible
smell went too.

13
Niffy Hatches a Plan

Ambrose was plodding through a field he had never been in before. He was not concerned by its unfamiliarity – it felt rather exciting – and, to his delight, he noticed he was surrounded by tall, lush dandelions. It was a bright, breezy day, and the Doe Child walked beside him, lead in hand, humming and chirping happily.

This, of course, was a dream, and Ambrose was very much enjoying it until an unpleasant

aroma invaded his nostrils. His nose twitched
so violently that it woke him with a start.

The smell was so bizarre that, spurred by
curious instinct alone, Ambrose flopped out
of bed and slipped through the door. With
one ear pointing straight up, one ear dragging
along the ground and his nose held high, he
followed the strange, acrid scent all the way
down the stairs.

Ambrose's nose led him from the foot of
the stairs to a room at the back of the house.
Jim's cottage was a ramshackle little thing,
and most of the wooden doors had warped
with old age. Luckily for Ambrose this meant
he could nudge this door open quite easily
with his nose.

It swung open and Ambrose could tell that
other animals had been in this room recently.
He could detect the distinctive scents of

house mice, small birds and — to his
disgust — cats.

All of these, though, were overpowered
by the bitter, intoxicating scent that had
awoken him. It seemed familiar, yet at the
same time was stronger than almost
anything he had smelt before. So strong,
in fact, that his eyes stung. So strong, it
was almost as if he could *see* the
smell.

He lolloped closer to the source. It was
very bright and hot and seemed to dance
before his eyes. He had never seen, nor
sniffed, anything quite like it.

Ambrose's curiosity got the better of him,
and he nuzzled even closer.

'Ouch!' He jumped back. There was a pain
in his nose, a pain unlike anything he had
felt before. It was simultaneously sharp, hot

and throbbing, and Ambrose did not like
it one bit. He turned tail and ran away
from the horrid bright beast that had hurt his
nose.

He scrambled back through the door. His
instincts told him that whatever this thing
was, it was dangerous. He was about to make
a dash for the stairs when several things
happened.

'Ambro-o-ose . . .' A mysterious voice was
coming from the kitchen.

Ambrose ambled
towards it. The smell
hit him.

'Ambro-o-ose . . .'
A ginger snout was
poking through the cat
flap.

'Niffy!'

'Hello, chum. Thought I might find you here. Roly's awfully worried about you, you know. Are you quite all right?'

'Not really,' Ambrose said miserably. 'I've hurt my nose and my eyes sting and – and, Niffy, there's something *funny* in here.'

'Funny peculiar or funny ha-ha?' the snout replied.

'Definitely peculiar. It's all bright and hot and it's getting bigger. I tried to sniff it and now my nose is *agony*!'

'Oh,' Niffy said. 'Oh dear.' His snout twitched and he let out a splutter.

'Now I don't want to alarm you, Ambrose, my old mate, but by the sounds of it – and judging by all this smoke – it rather seems your human's house is on fire.'

'Is that bad?' Ambrose enquired politely.

'Very,' Niffy said matter-of-factly. 'Tell you what, you go and wake up your kid and I'll make a big old racket out here.'

Ambrose didn't need to be told twice. He hopped to the stairs as fast as his short legs would carry him.

'And hurry!' Niffy called. 'Else you'll all be toast . . .'

Niffy had a plan.

He ran to the aviary. All was silent within.

' 'Scuse me? Hello?' He butted his head against the wire. Eventually he barked, 'Oi!'

Many pairs of beady eyes swivelled towards him.

'Croikey!' screeched a budgie with a bright green breast. 'Look it thit, boys. A fox!'

'That's me!' Niffy said cheerfully. 'Wonder if you fellows could help me out actually?'

He flashed them what he hoped was a friendly grin.

'What dost tha want wi' us?' said a small canary, who was as orange as Niffy himself.

'Need some help for my friend. He lives in that shed over there. White fur with grey patches. Got one ear that stands up and one that hangs down.'

'Aw yih,' trilled another greenish bird. 'Embrose, ya mean?'

'The very same!'

A chorus of shrill laughter broke out.

'Pull the other one, mite,' squawked another budgie. 'Rebbuts don't make frinds with foxes!'

'Tha'll be after t'poor lad,' a canary added grimly.

'Oh no, chaps,' Niffy said. 'You've got this all wrong. I don't want to *eat* him. In fact, I couldn't even if I wanted to.' He smiled widely to reveal the expanse of gum where his teeth should be. 'You see, he's stuck in your human's house. But the thing is – well, it's on fire.'

'Ee by gum!'

'Strewth! Not Embrose! He's a dinkum little rebbut!'

'Well, don't worry, I've got a plan,' Niffy replied. 'It's pretty simple actually. We just need to make as much noise as possible. And, no offence, but I know that's something you lot are good at.'

The birds cooed in agreement.

'On my count then, folks?'

Using his long snout as a conductor uses a baton, Niffy gave the signal, and soon the air was filled with a cacophony of shrieking, hollering and screeching.

For the second time that night Biddy opened her eyes with a start. She wasn't sure what woke her first – the velvety face butting her own or the raucous birdsong coming from outside.

At once she knew something was wrong. Ambrose pressed his nose urgently against her own again and the caterwauling continued.

Rising from the bed, she swept her rabbit up in her arms. She raced down the stairs and noticed the dining-room door, which hung open.

Biddy sensed several things at once. She heard her father snoring, felt her eyes smart from the smoke, tasted burning at the back of her throat and saw flames licking up the wall.

Cradling Ambrose close to her chest, she opened her mouth and at the top of her lungs screamed, 'FIRE!'

14

Au Revoir, Ambrose

Nobody fancied a cooked breakfast the next morning nor toast.

'The main thing,' said Mona, nibbling a banana, 'is that no one got hurt.'

'Speak for yourself, Mum!' Biddy replied indignantly. 'Ambrose's poor nose is all singed.'

'The hero of the hour,' Jim said thoughtfully.

He wasn't wrong. Thanks to Ambrose, Biddy had raised the alarm quickly enough to wake the whole house and put out the fire before too much harm was done. There was a large scorch mark up the wall of the dining room, though. 'Gives it a bit of character,' Jim had said.

'I told you he had the most amazing sense of smell,' Biddy said.

'Yes,' said Jim. 'Fancy smelling that from all the way out in the hutch!' He winked at his niece.

She looked down at her bowl sheepishly. 'I know I shouldn't have brought him inside, Uncle Jim,' she gabbled, 'and I'm ever so sorry, but he did turn out to be a lot of help in the end! I just wanted to give him a big cuddle before – before we have to leave today.'

Now it was Jasper's turn to look down at his bowl sheepishly.

He had not said much all morning. Though the cause of the fire had been no one's fault – a faulty plug socket – he felt guilty that he had not  woken up himself, and was rather shaken at the thought of what could have happened had Ambrose not smelt the burning.

'Don't fret, Biddy, love,' Jim said. 'Like I said, I'll build Ambrose a nice hutch of his own and he'll be here whenever you come to visit.'

'Perhaps he'll even have learnt some new tricks by the next time you see him, darling,' Mona added.

Biddy did not reply. She felt tears well in her eyes and quickly rubbed them away with her hand. 'May I leave the table now? I want to say *au revoir* to Ambrose.'

'*Au revoir*, dear?'

'Yes, Mum. It means "till I see you again". You ought to know that.'

And with that she hopped off her chair and strode out of the kitchen.

The thing Archibald liked best about Ambrose's extraordinary nose was that his brother could predict, seconds before they came into view, precisely which edible offerings the humans would be bringing that day.

Ambrose held his quivering nose aloft. He could smell mint and the other unique combination of scents that told him the Doe

Child was visiting alone. A fresh grassy scent wafted alongside.

'Celery!' he called to his brother.

'Oh, yippee,' said Archie, bouncing and then twisting in mid-air (which is what bunnies do when they are happy or excited).

The Doe Child unlatched the shed, dragging her feet slightly along the floor. She held a small bouquet of celery under her arm. With a long sigh (which is what humans do when they are sad or exhausted), she snapped off a stick of celery and poked it through the wire of Roland's hutch.

Then she opened the hutch that housed the five smaller rabbits, four of whom were not so small as they had been when she had met them the week before, and set down the rest of the celery. Archie pounced on it.

With one hand Biddy carefully picked Ambrose up and held him to her chest. With the other she petted each of his siblings in turn.

'Goodbye, kittens – although you're not really kittens any more. I hope you find some nice new humans to look after you.'

She stroked Woodsmoke between her neat little ears. '*Au revoir*, Woodsmoke. I hope you get some peace and quiet now.'

She closed the hutch door and held Ambrose up to her face so that their noses were almost touching. The two pairs of brown eyes met.

A tear slid down Biddy's cheek and Ambrose nuzzled into it. She opened her mouth as if to speak, but at that moment there was a quiet knock and the shed door was pushed open.

Ambrose, of course, had been able to smell another human approaching, although he had to admit it was a relatively odourless one. It smelt clean and slightly minty, though it was a subtly different kind of mint to the one Ambrose was used to smelling on Biddy.

'May I hold Ambrose, the world's first tracker rabbit?' Biddy's father said.

Bemused, Biddy nodded and passed the rabbit over. Jasper held him up to his face. A pair of brown and a pair of greeny-brown, bottom-of-the-duck-pond-coloured eyes met.

'He's rather handsome in a funny sort of way,' Jasper murmured. 'Does his nose ever stop wiggling?'

Biddy smiled sadly and shook her head.

Jasper handed back the rabbit, put his arm round his daughter and gave her a squeeze. 'You like helping Uncle Jim look after all his animals, don't you, Biddy? And you know what a big responsibility it is.'

'Obviously, Dad! It's pretty much all we've done all week, you know. As well as all the cooking and gardening and cycling and sewing and – well, you know what I mean.'

'I'm not sure how Jim fits it all in,' Jasper said, grinning. 'You know I don't much like animals, Biddy. Jim always wanted pets and I couldn't get my head round it. But I suppose that doesn't mean you should have to miss out.'

'Do you mean what I think you mean?' Biddy asked, trying to keep her voice level.

'I mean . . . well, do you still want to take Ambrose home with us?'

'More than anything!' Biddy cried. 'Really, Dad, can we really take him home?'

'Really,' he said. 'He's rather earned his keep, don't you think?'

'Yes!' Biddy replied.

'Perhaps,' Jasper said, 'one day we could get another rabbit, and she and Ambrose will

have baby rabbits, and we'll have a whole
team of tracker rabbits!'

'Steady on, Dad!' Biddy giggled. 'And a
baby rabbit is called a kitten, by the way.'

Her father chuckled. 'Good to know. Now,
we'd better get repacking the car, hadn't we?'

15
Pet Shop Day

From the top of her hutch in Rabbit Hall Woodsmoke had a clear view on to Jim's drive. She had been watching closely all morning and had seen the humans arranging various objects into the two cars. This was a routine she had seen many times before.

'Roland!' she called.

No answer came. She tried again.

He shuffled to the front of his hutch. 'Yes, sweetpea? My dearest dear, you called?'

'The Humans are packing up their cars. I think today might be – you know – pet shop day.'

Roland peered at Woodsmoke with his red eyes. 'Already, my darling? It seems like it comes round quicker each time, don't you think?'

'Not really,' Woodsmoke said shortly. 'But you don't have to share a hutch with them.'

'Eminently true, my love.'

Roland gave three thumps of his hind foot and cleared his throat. He tossed one ear over his shoulder in preparation for conversation.

The four young
rabbits looked up at
their father.

'Gather round,
kittens, for I have some
important information
to impart.' He spoke in

his deepest, most authoritative tones. 'Your
mother suspects that the time of your
departure may be imminent. Soon you will
make the journey every young rabbit must
undertake when they reach a certain age –
the journey to the pet shop.'

There was an awed silence. The earnest
expressions on her siblings' faces made Roly
want to giggle.

'You are mature enough now to make your
own way in the world, just as your mother
and I did when we were your age. Why, I

remember the day, it was a summer's day like today if I recall –'

'Roland.' Woodsmoke gave a little cough. 'Time is of the essence, remember.'

'Yes, yes, quite right, my dear,' Roland blustered. 'Soon, children, the Human will take you to a pet shop. There you will live temporarily until a new human is selected to care for you.'

'Will it be a large human or a child human?' April asked.

'Can't know for certain, my girl. You shall just have to wait and see,' Roland said.

'Will the new humans be as nice as these ones?' asked Ambrose.

'Oh yes, I'm sure they will serve quite well. Humans that like us rabbits tend to be a good sort.'

'I'll never find one as nice as the Doe Child, I bet,' Ambrose mumbled.

For the first time in his life Woodsmoke detected a note of petulance in her son's voice. 'Don't worry, dear, I'm sure you will,' she said.

'Dad,' said Archie, 'will my new humans have carrots?'

'Yes, Archibald, I'm sure your new servants will provide ample carrots,' Roland boomed.

'Are you absolutely *sure* there'll be carrots? And celery? And those scrummy little wheaty whatchamacallits?'

'The point is, kits,' Woodsmoke went on, 'your father and I are very proud of the young rabbits you've become, and we'll miss you terribly. But this is a very exciting time! Don't you think?'

She gazed at the four furry faces staring up at her. At least one of them, April, looked excited. Archie looked, as usual, somewhat confused. Ambrose looked very downhearted. Roly looked like she was plotting something.

'Mum,' she said, 'will we live in hutches like this with our new humans? Or will we be able to roam free?'

'Roam free!' Roland scoffed. 'You're no wild hare, Roly. You're a bunny, my girl, and you'll live in a hutch.'

Roly shot her father a very dark look. 'I won't,' she muttered quietly enough that Roland was not aware that she had said anything at all.

Woodsmoke had a feeling that her smallest kit would be proven right.

*

After much consulting with Jim about
exactly all the things Ambrose would need
for his new home, the car was packed.
Ambrose was settled in a newspaper-lined
crate stuffed with plenty of hay, water and a
carrot.

'Are you sure he's comfortable enough,
Biddy?' Jasper asked.

Patiently Biddy replied, 'He's fine, Dad —
look how happy he is!'

She was quite right, for Ambrose was
purring in that curious clackety way that
rabbits do when in a state of blissful
contentment. As if he knew he was being
watched, he flicked one eye open in a sort of
wink.

'Bye now, Ambrose,' Jim said,
scratching him on the head. 'See you again,
I'm sure.'

Biddy reached up to hug her uncle one last
time. 'Thank you, Uncle Jim,' she whispered.
'That was the best holiday ever.'

'You must come and visit us now, Jim, so
you can check up on your tracker rabbit,'
Mona said, hugging him once more.

'Yes, do visit, Jim,' Jasper added.

'Oh, you know me,' said Jim. 'Can't be away much. Got to stay here to look after the animals.'

'It's not far, Uncle Jim! You could just visit for the day sometimes.' Biddy's face lit up. 'And we could make the summer pudding again!'

'Now there's an offer you can't refuse,' Jasper said, smiling.

Jim grinned back at his brother, and then at Mona, and then at Biddy.

'You know, I think I will,' he said.

And, though Jim Johnson was a creature of habit by nature, he thought he would.

16
Rather Clever for a Rabbit

Jim's cottage seemed very quiet without
Biddy – not because she was a loud child, but
because they hardly ever stopped chattering
when they were together. Now he made the
short journey to Rabbit Hall in silence.

He had called the pet shop and arranged to
drop off three young rabbits that afternoon.
In truth, the only reason he had kept the litter
this long was so that Biddy could meet them.

He opened Woodsmoke's hutch. 'Hello, old girl,' he said to her. 'Getting crowded in here, isn't it?'

It wasn't, strictly speaking – not with Ambrose gone – but it soon would be at the rate the other young buck was growing.

Jim reached in and retrieved first the grey-blue buck and then the white doe, lowering them carefully into a box.

Woodsmoke gave a little chirrup.

'Now then,' Jim said, addressing her. 'Where's that lilac runt?'

He looked in the bottom of Woodsmoke's hutch. Then he peered in the top. He upended the food bowl and rummaged in the straw. There was no sign of another rabbit.

Jim regarded Woodsmoke. 'Funny, I could've sworn she was here earlier. Where's your doe, Woodsmoke?'

She fixed him with a blank stare.

'Must've got out again. We'll keep an eye out for her, shall we?'

The pretty grey rabbit looked back at him calmly and cocked her head.

Perhaps she knows something I don't, he thought. He shook his head as he closed the door to Rabbit Hall. *No, rabbits just aren't that clever.*

On the hill above Jim's cottage a pair of companions perched.

'You're rather clever for a rabbit, aren't you?' said Niffy.

'Oi!' Roly said indignantly. 'But, yes, actually I think I am.'

'Your mum must have eaten something funny when she was pregnant with you lot, what with Ambrose's nose and your vanishing skills. Are your other siblings quite normal?'

'Sort of,' said Roly. 'Although Archie has a pretty abnormal appetite.'

The old fox looked at the young rabbit. 'Won't you miss them? Your family?'

'They were annoying at times,' Roly replied, 'but I shall miss them. Ever so much.'

In the distance she could see – for rabbits are sometimes better at seeing objects that are far away than those that are up close – the shed in which her mother and father still lived. 'But I just couldn't bear the thought of living in a hutch forever. The others like it – you know, the bunny rabbit life – but I don't.'

'You have a real appreciation for freedom,' Niffy said fondly. 'You like to stop and smell the roses.'

'I prefer to stop and eat the dandelions actually.'

The fox chuckled. Roly looked up at him and he gave a kindly, if toothless, grin. They made an odd pair, she knew. One large, red and bristly with a big brush tail, and one very small, lilac and fluffy, with a round little tail.

'Are you sure you don't mind me tagging along with you, Niffy?'

'Course not! I think we share some of the same interests, you and I. And, truth be told, I don't have any foxy friends round here any more.'

'Suits me,' said Roly.

'Indeed it does! So, Roly the wild rabbit, where shall we explore first?'

'Anywhere!' Roly said. 'And everywhere.'

'Within reason,' said the fox, surveying the fields that stretched out in front of them. The sun was beginning to set.

'Within reason,' Roly agreed. She suddenly felt so overcome with happiness that she leapt in the air, did a little wriggle and landed neatly.

'You're full of beans!' said Niffy excitedly, and he too bounced skywards and let out a yap. Foxes, you see, are crepuscular creatures too.

They began to descend the hill, leaping and bounding and chasing each other's tails.

'You know, Roly, I've a feeling we'll see young Ambrose again.'

'I expect so,' she said thoughtfully. 'Mum says the Doe Child visits here quite often.'

'Plus,' said Niffy, 'he'll be able to sniff us out whenever he likes.'

'Oh yes,' Roly said, grinning to herself. 'He certainly will.'

A Note on the Authors

I was born in 1995, the Chinese Year of the Pig, and also the year in which the film *Babe* was released. My great-grandmother and great-grandfather went to see it at the cinema. At the time they had no idea how successful it would turn out to be.

My great-grandfather happens to be a wonderful writer called Dick King-Smith. (That's me pictured with him above, along with my dad, Tom, and my gran, Liz.) *Babe* was adapted from a book he wrote called *The Sheep-Pig*. His books only got more popular after that, and my childhood was full of them.

In fact, I like to think I gave him the idea for at least one of them, a story called *Lady Lollipop*. I remember telling him that he should write a story about a princess who wants a pet pig but isn't allowed one. So he did! And if you're an avid fan, you might remember a character in one of his later books with my name.

I've been writing stories and poems since I was very small too. Dick King-Smith, or Grampa Dick as I knew him, encouraged me to publish my first piece of writing when I was seven or eight. It was a silly poem – his favourite kind – called 'How to Get Comfy with an Anvil on Your Head'.

In the spring of 2020 I got an email from my great-uncle Giles. My gran, Liz, had found an unfinished story in her attic. Not just any old story, of course – Grampa Dick had started writing it many years ago. Giles told me that he and Liz and my great-aunt Juliet wanted to try to publish it, but the story didn't really have a proper ending. They asked if I would try to write one.

I cautiously agreed to give it a go and was promptly sent the manuscript. I enjoyed going through Grampa's typewritten, smudged and scribbled-on chapters – it felt a bit like getting to spend time with him again, even though he passed away in 2011 when I was sixteen.

I liked meeting these new yet familiar characters too, but I knew what my family meant about the story not having an ending. It stopped quite abruptly and I was left wondering what would happen to Ambrose and his nose and his intrepid human friend Biddy. It was funny (funny peculiar, I mean) realizing that *I* would get to decide!

Before I tried to finish this story, I knew I needed to study Grampa's other books. I think I've read almost all of them at some point in my life (there are over a hundred!), but this time I looked for patterns and quirks, and mapped out the plots. I looked closely at his words too, noticing how he constructed his jokes and sentences. I noted down silly words and phrases that were familiar to me because we use them in our family, but that writers now might not use.

The more I researched, the more my ideas grew. I knew that I wanted to add in some new characters – perhaps you can guess which ones! I was very excited when I eventually started writing, and I worked on the book all summer. I got to talk over plot ideas that I wasn't sure about with my friends, which is what Grampa used to do with my great-granny Myrle at the end of each writing day.

I was lucky that I could call Liz and Juliet and Giles whenever I needed advice about animals, family history or Woodlands Farm. Woodlands Farm is where they grew up, and it bears more than a passing resemblance to Jim's cottage in this story. I often thought about Dick and Myrle's house when I was writing too. I remember it being a wonky sort of cottage with a beautiful green garden.

After several months of writing, I was finished. I really hoped that my family would think the story was good enough. Taking over the story of a very successful writer is a lot of pressure! But by the time I typed the final words, I was proud of the story I had come up with. I don't think it's exactly what Grampa Dick would have written, but I think he would like it. I hope you like it too!

Josie Rogers
Glasgow, 2021